The Pee Wee Jubilee

The
Pee Wee
Jubilee

JUDY DELTON

Illustrated by Alan Tiegreen

A YEARLING BOOK

Published by
Bantam Doubleday Dell Books for Young Readers
a division of
Bantam Doubleday Dell Publishing Group, Inc.
1540 Broadway
New York, New York 10036

ISBN: 0-440-40226-3

Printed in the United States of America

September 1989

10 9 8

CWO

For Joan King, Kelly, and Katie,
with love

And with thanks to Lori Mack, editor

Contents

CHAPTER 1

Mrs. Peters's Big News

"**M**rs. Peters, Roger's putting leaves down my neck!" shouted Patty Baker.

Molly Duff leaned on her rake. "Roger really likes Patty," she said to her best friend, Mary Beth Kelly. "Nobody ever puts leaves down my neck."

The Pee Wee Scouts were having their Tuesday meeting in the park. They were raking the leaves and picking up litter.

"This whole meeting is one big good

deed," said Rachel Meyers. "I thought meetings were supposed to be fun."

"It's our civic duty," said Kevin Moe.

"Duty cootie," said Rachel. "My mom said I could rake at home. But since I'm here, she has to pay a boy to do it."

"We have to take care of our town," said Kevin. Kevin wanted to be mayor someday.

Mrs. Peters clapped her hands. She was their leader. The leader of Troop 23.

"Let's just put these piles into bags," she said, pushing the hair off her forehead. "Then we'll go back to my house and have a treat. And I'll tell you my good news."

"A treat?" said Roger White. "I hope it's something to drink. I'm thirsty."

"Good news?" said Molly. "I wonder what it is."

"Maybe Mrs. Peters is going to have another baby," said Lisa Ronning.

Molly looked at Mrs. Peters. She didn't look fat. "She just had a baby," she said. "You can't have another baby, one on top of another."

"Yes, you can," said Mary Beth. "My cousin was only ten months old when my aunt got another baby."

Baby Nick bounced up and down in his stroller. "Goo!" he said. He had a new tooth. He was drooling. All over the front of his jacket.

"Well, Nick isn't ten months old yet," said Molly in relief. She didn't want Mrs. Peters to have any more babies. If she did she might decide she didn't have time to be a troop leader. She might have to spend more time making baby cereal. And buying those little plastic educational toys so the baby wouldn't be dumb.

After all, Molly was an only child. Only children were fine. One was enough for Mrs. Peters.

Kenny Baker held a trash bag open for leaves. But instead, Sonny Betz took a huge jump and landed inside it. Kenny pretended to close the bag and tie it up and drag it away. The bag yelled, "Hey! Let me out of here!" Then it jumped up and landed on Kenny and wrestled him to the ground.

Mrs. Peters clapped her hands again. "What did we learn about plastic bags?" she said.

"You can suffocate," said Tracy Barnes. Sonny stuck his head out of the bag.

"Let's finish up," said Rachel. "I want to know about the news."

The Pee Wees bagged all the leaves. Then they got into Mrs. Peters's van and headed back to her house for the end of the meeting. "Everyone buckle up," she said.

"I'll bet the news is a party," said Tim Noon.

"Maybe it's a new mascot," said Tracy.

"We've already got a mascot. We've got Lucky," said Lisa.

Lucky was waiting for them at Mrs. Peters's house. He had grown into a big dog since the Scouts got him.

"I think," said Mary Beth, "that the news is a contest. A Pee Wee Scout contest. Whoever has the most good deeds wins a car."

"Ho, ho," Roger laughed. "Hey, Mary Beth, I'll take a Corvette. A red one!" He chuckled.

Soon all the boys were making engine noises. And holding make-believe steering wheels.

"Varooooom!" shouted Tim.

"My uncle won a car in a contest," said Mary Beth. She looked hurt.

"How many good deeds did he do?" Roger shouted. "Did he get a driving badge?" Roger bent over laughing.

"The news could be a contest," said Molly to Roger. "We could win a car. Mrs. Peters could drive it."

"Goo!" said Nick.

"See, Nick thinks so too!" cried Lisa.

"Here we are!" called Mrs. Peters, stopping the van in her driveway. "All out for some refreshments."

The Pee Wees tumbled out of the van. They raced one another to the front door. They washed up and gathered around the big table in Mrs. Peters's basement. Mrs. Peters put baby Nick to bed for a nap.

"Let's hear the news," demanded Kevin, hitting the table with his hand.

"Let's have our treat," said Roger.

Mrs. Peters poured milk into glasses. She got out some cans of soda pop. And she put some apples and oranges and grapes on the table. Molly carried in a tray of brownies.

"Yummm," said Mary Beth, rubbing her stomach. "I'm starving."

While the Pee Wees were munching, Mrs. Peters said, "My big news is about the Pee Wee Jubilee. It's far away, in Atlanta, Georgia. And guess what? We are all going!"

CHAPTER 2

That Jewel Thing

The Scouts stopped eating. They didn't say anything. They stared at their leader.

"In the ocean?" said Sonny. "Is it in the Atlanta Ocean?"

"I'm glad it isn't another baby," said Molly in relief.

"A party would have been better," said Tim.

Mrs. Peters laughed. "It is a party," she said. "A great big party."

The Pee Wees looked doubtful.

"A jubilee is like a party," Mrs. Peters explained.

"My mom wears that around her neck and on her arms and her fingers," said Sonny.

Mrs. Peters frowned. "I think you mean jewelry," she said. "A jubilee is a big festival. Pee Wee Scouts from all over the country come together for a weekend. They meet new friends and play games. They camp out in tents and learn how other Scouts live. They sing and go to meetings and find out what it means to be a Pee Wee Scout."

"We know what it means to be a Pee Wee Scout," said Sonny. "I don't want to go to that jewelry thing in the ocean."

"Atlanta is a big city," said Mrs. Peters.

Lisa raised her hand. "Do we get off school?" she asked.

Mrs. Peters shook her head. "It is from

Friday afternoon until Sunday night," she said. "You won't have to miss any school."

The Pee Wees groaned. They liked to miss school.

"I get homesick," said Sonny.

"That's the next good news," said Mrs. Peters. "Your parents come too. No one will get homesick. This is a family jubilee!"

"My mom and dad won't go," said Tracy. "Because of the baby."

"I talked to your mother about that, and they're able to come," said Mrs. Peters.

Mrs. Peters told them about the fun they would have with new Pee Wees. She talked about the games and crafts and bonfires and good food. Soon the Scouts got excited about the Jubilee. Before long even Sonny wanted to go.

"We have to label our belongings. And

make name tags. And make a banner for Troop 23."

"Can Lucky and Tiny come?" asked Kenny.

"No dogs allowed," said Mrs. Peters. "They will have to stay in a kennel."

"Arf!" said Tiny, Mrs. Peters's Labrador.

"Yip!" said Lucky.

The dogs ran in circles.

"Most of your parents know about this," said Mrs. Peters loudly. The dogs barked more. "But we wanted to surprise all of you with the news today."

"Yeah!" The Scouts cheered for the Pee Wee Jubilee.

They helped clean up the crumbs and dishes. Then they said their Pee Wee Scout pledge. After that they sang the Pee Wee Scout song.

"Put the last weekend of September on your calendar!" called Mrs. Peters as they left. "See you next week."

12

*   *   *

"It will feel scary to go so far from home," said Lisa.

"Naw," said Rachel. "It will be fun. I've been all the way to Hawaii. That's far."

"Weren't you scared?" asked Tracy.

"Nope," said Rachel. "And I flew on a plane too. Over the ocean."

"This will be more fun," said Patty. "Because all of us will go together."

Molly couldn't wait to get home and talk to her mom and dad about it. She waved to her friends and ran the rest of the way. She burst in the back door all out of breath.

"Guess what?" she said. Mrs. Duff was setting the table for dinner. "Mrs. Peters told us about the Pee Wee Jubilee. It's far away and the parents come too! We play games and sing and meet new Scouts and camp out."

Her mother laughed. "I know," she said. "We heard all about it."

14

Molly climbed up on the chair so she could reach the calendar. She circled the last weekend in September with a pencil. "This is when we go," she said.

Mrs. Duff looked at the calendar. She had a plate in one hand. "Oh, no!" she said. "It can't be that weekend. I thought it was the weekend before! That last weekend in September is Aunt Carol's wedding. Dad and I won't be able to go to the Jubilee if it's on the same day as the wedding."

"Why does she have to get married on the last Saturday in September? Why can't she change it?" said Molly. "Mom! You have to come! All the other parents will be there."

"I'm sorry, honey. We can't skip Aunt Carol's wedding. She's Daddy's sister."

"Tell Aunt Carol to get married the next week!" cried Molly. "Please?"

CHAPTER 3

Orphan Molly

Mrs. Duff put down the plate. "We can't change a wedding, Molly. Invitations are sent out and the church is reserved and the flowers are ordered."

Mrs. Duff ran into the living room to talk to Mr. Duff. Then they both looked at the calendar again.

"I thought the Jubilee was the middle weekend in September," he said.

They thought and thought about what

to do. Finally Molly's father said, "Well, we can't miss my sister's wedding."

"You can't miss the Jubilee!" cried Molly.

"You can go anyway." said Mrs. Duff. "I am sure Mary Beth's family won't mind if you go with them. Or Lisa's. I'll bet even Mrs. Betz would be glad to have a little girl for a weekend."

Mrs. Betz! Be Mrs. Betz's little girl?

Oh, no!

Molly ran to her room. She didn't feel like eating dinner. She would be the only Scout without parents. Molly cried into her pillow.

Soon she heard her mother at the door.

"You don't have to go with the Betzes," Mrs. Duff said softly. "I called Mrs. Kelly. You can go with Mary Beth. Won't that be fun?"

Molly nodded. She didn't mind the Kellys. But it wouldn't be the same as

17

having her own parents with her. She would be an orphan! Homeless. Someone extra. Everyone would point to her and say, Her mom and dad couldn't come.

The next morning on the playground, Mary Beth came running up to Molly.

"You're going with me!" she said, jumping up and down. "We'll be like sisters!"

Mary Beth put her arm around Molly. Molly felt confused. How could she complain about being an orphan in front of Mary Beth?

Mary Beth was running all over the playground telling everyone the news.

"How come you aren't going with your own family?" asked Rachel.

Molly wanted to say, None of your beeswax. But instead she said, "My mom and dad have to go to a wedding. It's all planned."

"My dad canceled a business meeting," said Rachel.

"Well, you can't cancel a wedding," muttered Molly.

"You could come with my family," Lisa offered. "How come you didn't come with me? Do you like Mary Beth better than me?"

If Molly said she liked Lisa better, Mary Beth would be hurt. If she said she liked Mary Beth better, then Lisa would be hurt. This Jubilee thing was getting off on the wrong foot.

"My mom made the plans," said Molly.

At recess Tracy said, "You could have come with my family."

After school Sonny said, "I'm glad you didn't have to come with me."

Molly wished she didn't have to go at all. Maybe she should go to her aunt's wedding instead. But Mrs. Peters wouldn't like that. And besides, weddings were dull.

*   *   *

Soon it was Tuesday and time for another Pee Wee Scout meeting.

"Guess what?" said Mrs. Peters, smiling. "I have some more news!"

Oh, no, thought Molly. More trouble.

"We had planned to drive to the Jubilee," said Mrs. Peters. "But it is so far away that we found we would need more days than we have. So guess what we are going to do?"

"Stay home?" said Tim.

Mrs. Peters laughed and shook her head.

"Take a bus!" said Kenny.

"A boat!" said Sonny.

"No." Mrs. Peters laughed. "We are going to fly. I have worked things out with your parents and we got the tickets at a bargain rate, so we are all going on a big jet."

"Big deal," scoffed Rachel. "I fly all the time."

21

None of the other Scouts had ever been in an airplane.

"Whoopee!" shouted Roger, sailing around the room with his arms out like wings. "A jet!"

"Zooooom!" went Kevin. Soon all the boys were making airplane noises.

"We have to fly over many states," said Mrs. Peters above the noise. "But we will get there quickly by plane. Then we will have more time to enjoy the Jubilee."

Things were happening too fast for Molly.

A jubilee.

A new family.

A trip without her parents.

And her first ride on an airplane.

Sonny began to cry. "There are too many of us," he cried. "The plane will fall!"

"Dummy," said Roger. "Planes hold millions of people. Even fat people."

"Planes fly all the time without falling. And your mother will be with you," said Mrs. Peters.

Molly was disgusted. She was glad she wasn't going with the Betzes.

During the rest of the meeting the Scouts planned what to take. They made a Troop 23 banner to carry. They made a big poster too. It said PEE WEE SCOUT TROOP 23 at the top. The rest of the poster had photographs pasted all over it. Pictures of the Pee Wees playing football and softball and doing good deeds.

"We want to show the other Scouts what our troop does here in our town. And at the Jublilee we will find out what the other troops do," said Mrs. Peters.

When they finished the poster, she passed out paper that was sticky on one side to make name tags.

"We will wear these name tags on the plane and the whole time we are at the

Jubilee," she said. "Then everyone will learn your name."

Suddenly Rachel waved her hand. "Mrs. Peters! Mrs. Peters! Molly wrote *Molly Duff*. Shouldn't she write *Molly Kelly* because she will be part of the Kelly family at the Jubilee because her parents can't come?"

"Her name is still Molly Duff, Rachel," said Mrs. Peters.

Molly stuck her tongue out at Rachel.

After the name tags were finished, Mrs. Peters talked about how to act on a plane. About the seat belts and the safety rules. About the rest rooms and trays for dinner. About not running in the aisles.

"How can they cook on a plane?" asked Patty.

"They even show movies," said Rachel.

"How can they do all that up in the air?" asked Tracy.

Mrs. Peters answered all of their questions. Then she talked more about the Jubilee.

The Scouts were so excited, they could not think of any good deeds they had done that week.

They said the Pee Wee Scout pledge and sang their song. They cleaned up the paper and scraps and got ready to leave.

"It will be time to go before you know it," said Mrs. Peters. "Next week we will be off to the Pee Wee Jubilee!"

CHAPTER 4

Pie in the Sky

Mrs. Peters was right. The Jubilee weekend came fast.

"You'll have a good time," said Mr. Duff. "Just be careful and mind the Kellys and don't talk to strangers."

She'd have to talk to strangers, thought Molly. Almost everyone she would meet at the Jubilee would be a stranger.

"Beep, beep!" went a car horn outside. It was the Kellys. Molly's mother kissed her. Her dad gave her a hug. Molly strapped her backpack on and waved good-bye.

Mary Beth was bouncing up and down in the backseat.

The Kellys waved to the Duffs and then they started for the airport. When they got there Mr. Kelly parked the car in the weekend parking lot, and they hurried to gate 5. The first Scout they saw was Sonny.

"I don't want to go on a plane!" he shrieked.

"Everyone hold up your tickets," Mrs. Peters was saying.

Everyone did. Even the parents.

Over the loudspeaker a deep voice announced their flight.

"Leaving at gate 5," the voice said.

"We're ready!" shouted Roger. "I hope I get to sit by a window."

"I'd like to ride on the wings," said

Kevin. "Like these guys in this movie I saw on TV. They had parachutes."

Sonny wailed even louder. Mrs. Betz picked him up and carried him, like a piece of baggage, under her arm. Sonny kicked. And struggled. But soon he was on the plane.

"No pushing," called Mrs. Peters. "Your parents will find your seat number on your boarding pass."

"Hey, I've got a window seat!" shouted Roger.

"I want to sit by Patty!" shouted Lisa.

"Let's all sit with our families until we are in the air," said Mrs. Peters.

Molly sat next to Mary Beth. Mr. and Mrs. Kelly sat behind them.

"The wings are going to fall off!" shouted Sonny. "Look how loose they are."

"Let's put all our baggage under the seat in front of us," said Mrs. Peters.

"Mine won't fit," said Tracy. She pushed

and shoved, but her bag was too big. Her mother tried to get it under the seat, but it didn't fit.

"Remember we were all to bring only one small bag," said Mrs. Peters. "What is in there, Tracy?"

"It's my teddy bear," she answered. "I can't sleep without him."

Tracy's mother looked embarrassed. "I didn't know you took Freddie," she said.

Finally Mrs. Peters put the bag with the bear in the luggage rack over the seats.

The flight attendant showed the Scouts how to fasten their seat belts.

Then she showed them the emergency exits. And how to use the life jackets.

And the oxygen masks.

"These seats we are sitting on can float," said Rachel, combing her hair. "If we crash into the ocean, our cushion floats like a little boat."

Sonny, who had been quiet, began to howl all over again.

"It's going to fall," he cried. "Help!"

"It is not," said Mrs. Betz.

"Then why do the cushions float?" he sobbed.

Mrs. Betz glared at Rachel.

All of a sudden there was a loud noise. The engine had started.

The plane began to move.

It rolled down the runway.

Sonny's face was buried in his mother's lap. The engine made so much noise, they couldn't hear Sonny crying.

The plane went faster and faster! Molly leaned back in her seat and held on to the armrests. Her stomach began to feel queasy. Was she going to throw up? She had no mother to hold her hand. To take her to the bathroom. She couldn't even go to the bathroom alone, because she was strapped in! She'd have to use

that little bag in the pocket in front of her.

"Mama!" cried Sonny.

Just when she was sure she would throw up, Molly seemed to calm down. She looked out the window. The houses and cars outside were smaller. And then they disappeared. All Molly could see was clouds. Clouds and more clouds.

"Maybe this is what heaven looks like," said Tracy.

"I don't see any of those angels with the wings and the white bathrobes," said Tim. "And none of those guys playing guitars."

All the Scouts laughed.

Sonny heard the laughing and opened one eye. "Are we falling?" he asked.

"Of course not," said Mrs. Betz. "It's a nice smooth flight."

"Guitars," scoffed Roger. "Where would they plug them in? Everybody knows they only play banjos in heaven."

Rachel sighed. "They play harps," she said. "Angels play harps."

Molly's stomach felt better. Now that the plane seemed to stay in the sky, she even felt hungry. Smells of food filled the air.

Soon a lady came down the aisle pushing a cart with little trays on it. Each tray held a salad, a hamburger and bun, and french fries. Little tiny cups held pickles and olives and ketchup and mustard. And on a little dish of its own was a tiny piece of apple pie.

"Pie in the sky," chuckled Roger.

The lady with the cart said her name was Sally. She showed the Scouts how to pull the tray table down in front of them and set their food on it.

Suddenly a voice sounded overhead.

"It's God," whispered Tracy.

"It's the pilot," scoffed Roger.

"This is your captain speaking," the

voice said. "We are experiencing a little turbulence. We will soon pass out of it. Please fasten your seat belts."

"Why?" said Sonny, with mustard on his face. "In case we fall in the ocean?"

"We're nowhere near an ocean," said Rachel, paging through her airline magazine.

"She's brave," said Mary Beth.

"She's a show-off," said Lisa.

By the time the trays were cleared away Sonny felt better. And Molly was enjoying her cozy seat by the window. Mrs. Peters led the Scouts in a sing-along, ending up with the Pee Wee Scout song. As they finished they heard the voice again.

"In five minutes we will be landing," it said. "Please put your seats in an upright position and fasten your seat belts. Thank you for flying with Ace Airways."

The seat belts went click, click, click.

The plane went down, down, down.

"Look!" shrieked Molly. "I can see houses again. And little cars."

The cars and houses got bigger and bigger.

"We're going in the river!" shouted Kevin.

But the plane slipped over the river onto the runway on the other side. With a tiny bump the wheels touched the ground. The engine roared as the plane slowed down. Then it came to a full stop.

Mrs. Peters and the parents stood up. They gathered the luggage.

Sally waved good-bye, and everybody plowed through the door, down the walkway, and into the airport. Mrs. Kelly held Mary Beth's hand on one side and Molly's on the other.

They walked into the big Atlanta airport.

"This place is ten miles long!" Kevin whistled.

"Look at all the Scouts!" cried Molly.

There were fat Scouts, thin Scouts.

Black Scouts, white Scouts.

Scouts with braids and Scouts with curls.

Some troops had green kerchiefs.

Some had purple and some had blue.

Some had badges all over their shirts!

Everywhere Molly looked there were Pee Wee Scouts.

She could see banners that said IDAHO, and CALIFORNIA, and NEW YORK. There were Scouts from Hawaii with leis around their necks.

"There's Troop 15!" shouted Tim. Some of the Pee Wees from Oakdale turned around. They wore blue kerchiefs.

Suitcases, tents, and backpacks were propped up against the wall. The airport was packed with Scouts!

"Well, I guess we aren't the only Pee Wee Scouts in town," said Kevin.

Mrs. Peters smiled. "Kevin is right. We aren't the only troop around."

Molly shivered. All these strange Pee Wees seemed to know what to do.

"This way!" called Mrs. Peters. She led them through the crowd to a door. It was warm and sunny outside. A big school bus was waiting.

"Hop on," said the driver. "And welcome to Atlanta, Georgia. Welcome to the Pee Wee Jubilee!"

"He talks funny, doesn't he?" said Molly to Lisa.

The bus drove through the city. The Scouts stared out the window.

"That building goes up to the sky." said Patty. "I can't see the top of it."

"There's no sky in Atlanta," said Tracy. "Only buildings."

"There will be sky when we get to the campsite," said Roger's father.

The driver drove and drove. Through the city. Onto a freeway.

"We're going to a forest," shouted Sonny. "I saw a tree!"

Just then the driver turned the bus off the freeway and into the woods. The road became narrow and bumpy. In the woods was a large clearing. Rows and rows of yellow school buses were there. Music was playing.

Molly felt butterflies in her stomach.

Roger whistled. "This place is bigger than the airport," he said.

The bus driver pulled on the brake and opened the door.

"Here we are," he called. "All out for the Pee Wee Jubilee!"

CHAPTER 5

A Million Pee Wees

"Look at all the tents," said Mary Beth as the Scouts got off the bus. "I'll bet there are about a million."

"And a million Pee Wees!" shouted Kevin.

"There's a lake," called Roger. "I didn't know there was a lake in Atlanta."

A big red banner stretched over their heads.

WELCOME, it said. PEE WEE CAMPSITE.

A million tents.

A million Pee Wees.

A lake inside a forest.

A forest inside a city.

Molly felt as if she were a million miles from home. From her school. From Mrs. Peters's cozy little house. From Troop 23 meetings. This was a giant Pee Wee Scout meeting.

After the Scouts had walked and walked, up one row of tents and down another, they came to a flag that said 23.

"Here we are!" called Mrs. Betz. "And we are near the lake."

The Scouts crawled into the tents with their parents. Molly crawled in with the Kellys. She sat down on a strange sleeping bag.

The Kellys were nice to her. They even loved her. But they weren't her own family.

Molly felt tired. And a little homesick.

"Isn't this fun?" said Mary Beth. "Don't you just love it here? Aren't we going to have a great time?"

Before Molly could answer, she had fallen asleep. Mrs. Kelly covered her with a blanket, and she didn't wake up until morning.

"You missed supper," said Mrs. Kelly in the morning. "I guess you were very tired from all the excitement."

Molly didn't feel so homesick now. The sun was shining. The camp didn't look scary. Neither did all the new Scouts. And Mrs. Kelly was the best mother an orphan could have. If you had to be an orphan.

"Today is a full day," said Mrs. Kelly. "Full of things to do. To start, we have a pancake breakfast."

The girls brushed their teeth and washed

and got dressed. Then they went through the woods and past rows of tents with Mr. and Mrs. Kelly. They went into a big building with a cement floor.

Roger was there with his father. They were already eating pancakes at a long table.

Soon the other Scouts started to come with their parents and their leaders. Before long the whole big hall was filled.

Someone hit a pie tin with a spoon and said, "Attention, please!" into a squeaky microphone. "Welcome to our first Pee Wee Jubilee," he said. "I am Mr. Reed, one of the chairmen on the Jubilee committee."

The Pee Wees looked bored. They wanted to eat pancakes. But Roger and Mr. White put their forks down.

"Before we eat our breakfast," Mr. Reed went on, "I'd like to ask each one of you to move to a table with Scouts you have not met. Leave your own troop and meet new friends. That is one of the goals of our Jubilee."

It was noisy as chairs shuffled on the floor. Pee Wees left their mothers and fathers and went to new tables.

"Hi, I'm Rachel, and I'm in Troop 23," said Rachel, reaching out her hand to a Scout with a lei around her neck. "I went to Hawaii once," she said.

Mrs. Kelly gave Molly and Mary Beth little shoves. "Now you two separate," she said. "Just for breakfast."

It was bad enough not having a mother. Now Molly had to leave her best friend.

Mrs. Peters started putting her Pee Wees at different tables. Molly sat down at a new table. A strange mother reached out her hand and said, "I'm Mrs. Lawson from Texas." She sounded funny, like the bus driver.

"I'm Molly," said Molly shyly.

There were four other Scouts at the table, but they were shy too. They didn't say anything. The parents talked to each other.

Soon big piles of pancakes were served. Mountains of pancakes. Molly loved pancakes. At home. Today she didn't feel like eating. She felt nervous, as if these new Scouts were all looking at her.

Soon the other Scouts began talking to one another. They even laughed. But they didn't talk to Molly. She tried to open her mouth to say something. But nothing came out.

Suddenly *all* the Scouts in the room were talking. They were laughing. They were making new friends.

All except Molly.

She saw Mary Beth talking to a Scout with an orange kerchief and lots of badges.

She saw Roger hit a strange Scout on the back in a friendly way.

Even Sonny was handing a piece of bacon to a girl across the table from him.

"Rat's knees," said Molly. "Everyone has a new friend but me."

When breakfast was over, Mr. Reed held up his hand for silence. "I see my trick worked," he said. "I see you all have new friends. Show me your new friend!" he shouted.

Hands went up over heads. Hands held together. They showed Mr. Reed their new friends.

Molly's hand was not up. She did not have a new friend.

"Let's take our new friend by the hand," said Mr. Reed, "and go to our first meeting of the day. These are the things you can choose to do."

He waved a piece of paper over his head. Parents handed papers out to every Scout. The papers had lists on them.

"Choose what you like the best," said

Mr. Reed into the microphone. "You can do wood carving, ceramics, pottery, or weaving. You can go on a nature hike, go fishing, run in a race. You decide. Get that Pee Wee Scout spirit going."

He punched the air with his fist. "Let's go!"

All the Scouts cheered, "Yeah!"

"I'm going fishing!" yelled Roger. "With my dad."

Fishing sounded like fun to Molly. But so did hiking. So did weaving. Pottery and ceramics too.

Lisa held her new friend by the hand. "We're going to weaving," she said. "Come with us."

Molly shook her head. She'd always wanted to make something nice out of clay. Something that lasted a long time. This might be her only chance.

She decided to go to the pottery class.

CHAPTER 6

A Bowl and a Buddy

Mr. Kelly showed Molly the way to the pottery tent. It was a big tent. It was open on the sides.

A lady who looked like a Scout leader stood in the tent smiling. She wasn't like Mrs. Peters.

Molly missed seeing Mrs. Peters up in front. She was the best leader of all. No one could be as good as Mrs. Peters.

"I'm Mrs. Morgan," said the new lady.

She had clay on her hands. And on her apron too. Pots and vases stood everywhere. And pottery wheels. The kilns were in the back.

"Come right in," she called to Molly.

There were a few Scouts already there. More Scouts came in, holding hands with new friends. Laughing and talking.

Molly looked at the pretty things on the tables.

A big blue vase.

A tiny salt shaker.

A holder for pipes.

Molly wished her dad smoked a pipe. It would be fun to make a pipe holder with her own hands and take it home to him. But a pipe holder was no good for a father who didn't have pipes.

When everyone was there, Mrs. Morgan showed them the wet shiny clay they would be using. She sat down at the pottery wheel. When she pressed the pedal

with her foot, the wheel began to spin. She threw a lump of clay on the wheel and shaped it with her hands as it went round and round.

Oh, boy! Molly couldn't wait to get her hands on that clay. She knew she could make something beautiful.

Round and round went Mrs. Morgan's wheel. The clay got smoother and smoother. Round and smooth.

Molly stood patiently with the others while Mrs. Morgan explained how to do it. "And when we are all through, we will bake it in the kiln," she said.

"Like a pie," said one of the Scouts.

"Like a baked potato," said a familiar voice. Molly looked around. It was Tracy!

Finally it was time to take turns. A boy named Hal threw his clay on a wheel. Some of it splattered in his face. The rest of it rode around on the wheel like a lump of dough.

"Shape it," said Mrs. Morgan to Hal. "Try to get your hands around it."

Hal put his hands on the clay. "I'm making a pitcher for orange juice," he said. But when he was finished he had a small flat dish.

"It can be a soap dish," said Mrs. Morgan kindly. "It's hard to make a pitcher when you are just beginning."

Molly waited for her turn.

A girl named Suzie started to make a candle holder. When she finished she said, "I changed my mind. I made a dogfood dish instead."

Molly knew what she wanted to make. A sugar bowl for her mother. A beautiful sugar bowl that could sit on the table all day. Everyone would see it. Her mother would say, Molly made this all by herself at the Jubilee.

Molly would put her name in the wet clay on the bottom so that everyone would know she had made it. It would last forever.

Finally it was Molly's turn. Everyone watched her. She placed her clay on the center of the wheel. She pressed her hands on it and shaped it as it went around. It felt so smooth.

The wheel turned and turned. Molly dipped her hands in a bowl of water. Then she held the clay. Round and round. The wheel hummed. Molly felt like humming too. She pressed the pedal more to make the wheel go faster.

"I think you have it!" said Mrs. Morgan. Molly took her foot off the wheel. She hated to let go of the smooth clay. But her sugar bowl was finished.

"It's lovely," said Mrs. Morgan. "You have a real gift, Molly. You are an artist."
* Molly put a blue glaze on her sugar bowl and put it into the kiln with the soap dish and the dogfood dish. One Scout made a cup without a handle and

another made a pencil holder that leaned to one side.

"Now," said Mrs. Morgan. "We have to wait for a while. You may have lunch and then go to one of the other activities. At the end of the day come back here and get your work."

Mrs. Morgan held up the sheet of paper with the activities on it. She looked at her watch. "You can go run in a race," she read, "or take a bus ride into Atlanta to see Peachtree Plaza, or take a boat ride on the lake."

Molly didn't want to see Peachtree Plaza. It was probably just a shopping mall. And she didn't want to run in a race. She just wanted to stay in the cool pottery tent and wait for her sugar bowl to finish baking.

But Molly ate lunch anyway. Then she went for a boat ride on the lake. She watched some Pee Wee Scouts play Capture the Flag. Then she dashed back to the pottery tent to see if her sugar bowl was ready.

Mrs. Morgan was just taking things out of the oven. "You are just in time, Molly."

She held up the sugar bowl for Molly.

It was light blue.

It was shiny.

It was the most beautiful sugar bowl Molly had ever seen.

Mrs. Morgan wrapped paper around the bowl. Then she put it in a little bag. She handed it to Molly with a smile. "I hope you make more nice things," she said.

Molly carried the bag carefully. She couldn't wait to get back to the tent to show the Kellys. Hop, skip, jump. Molly ran down the path between the tents.

All she could think about was clay. The things she could make now. Jars. Mugs. Vases. Toothbrush holders. Little animals.

Suddenly Molly noticed that all of the tents looked alike. Where was she? The flags in front of the tents had big numbers on them. 104. 56. 88. But no 23.

She stopped to look around. The flags flapped in the breeze. She saw rows of tents on her right. Rows of tents on her left. But where was Troop 23? Where was her tent with the Kellys?

Molly ran up one row and down another. "What a big place this is," she said out loud. Her stomach felt funny. She had a scary feeling. A feeling like she was lost. Tears came into her eyes. She felt a lump in her throat. Oh, no.

Molly walked on. She came to a path in the woods. Then she came to the lake. But it was a different part of the lake. Not the part where she went on the boat ride.

"Maybe I'll have to eat berries to stay alive!" she said. It seemed chilly outside. Would it be dark soon? Where were the Kellys? Where was the dining hall with Mr. Reed? And all those Scouts?

All of a sudden it was very quiet.

"Help, help!" called Molly. "I'm lost!"

No one answered. She sat down under a tree to rest. She held on to her sugar bowl tightly. What should she do?

She closed her eyes. She decided not to open them until she thought of what to do next.

"Hi," she heard someone say.

She opened her eyes.

A Scout with a round face looked at her. He had on glasses. Around his neck was a bright yellow scarf.

"Hi," he said again. "My name's Buddy. I'm in Troop 88. We're from Hollywood. Who are you?"

Hollywood?

Movie stars lived in Hollywood!

Molly jumped to her feet. "I'm Molly," she said. "I'm in Troop 23. And I can't find my tent."

"I'll show you my tent," said Buddy. "Follow me."

They hiked back to the long rows of tents. "I want to see what time supper is," he said.

Buddy looks like he likes to eat, thought Molly. His face was round. He was round all over.

"I know where the dining hall is," he added. "Do you know your way from the dining hall?"

Molly nodded. "If I saw the dining hall, I could run right to my tent," she said.

"Follow me," said Buddy again.

As Molly followed him, Buddy said, "See this belt?" He pointed to his waist. "I made it this morning. In weaving."

"It's nice," said Molly. "I made this."

Molly unwrapped her sugar bowl. She held it carefully while she walked.

"Wow!" said Buddy. "You made that yourself?"

Molly nodded.

"It's real good," he said. "Do you want to see my scrapbook? Our troop keeps scrapbooks."

"Sure," said Molly. "Are you a movie star?"

"Nope," said Buddy. "But my dad is a cameraman."

"Neat," said Molly.

Buddy went up one row of tents and down another. He turned a corner by a patch of dogwood, and there was the dining hall.

"Want to eat supper with my troop?" Buddy offered.

"I have to go back to my tent," said Molly. "But I'll see you afterward."

Molly waved to Buddy and ran toward her tent. The Troop 23 flag waved in front of it.

CHAPTER 7

Hold, Hold, Hold My Hand

"It's beautiful!" said Mary Beth when Molly showed her the sugar bowl.

"What a lovely color," said Mrs. Kelly. "You have a real eye for color, Molly."

Mrs. Kelly put the sugar bowl on a table where they all could admire it.

"We were worried about you," she said. "The pottery class was over and you didn't come back."

"I was lost," said Molly. "But a boy

66

from Troop 88 showed me the way back."
Molly told them about Buddy.

When Molly got to the dining hall,
Buddy was there with his scrapbook. "Our
whole troop makes these," he said.

"What a good idea," said Mrs. Kelly.
"We will have to tell Mrs. Peters about
them."

As Molly was looking at pictures of
Troop 88 selling Christmas wreaths, Sonny
came by. He squeezed in between Molly
and Buddy and the scrapbook.

"Look at those palm trees!" he said.
"Hey, where do you live, Hawaii?"

"It's Hollywood," said Molly proudly.
"This is Buddy. My friend."

"Hey, do you know any movie stars?"
asked Sonny.

"I met Benji once," said Buddy. "When
my dad shot him."

"Your dad shot Benji?" yelled Sonny.
"How could he shoot Benji?"

"With a camera," explained Buddy. "That's his job."

"Do you live by the ocean?" Sonny asked.

"No, but we've got a swimming pool," said Buddy. "A great big one."

"Wow!" said Sonny, putting his arm around Buddy. "I never knew anyone with his own swimming pool."

"My aunt's got a pool," said Rachel, who was across the table.

Mr. Reed was banging on a pan. "Your attention, please! Tomorrow we will choose the Pee Wee Scout of the Year! Please be thinking of who you will vote for."

"Did you hear that?" shouted Roger. "I think I should be Pee Wee Scout of the Year. I have lots of badges."

"I've got more," said Kevin. "I'll bet I win."

"You two had better campaign, then,"

said Roger's dad. "The way you win is to advertise. You need slogans too."

Roger went off to his tent. Kevin left too.

After supper, when Molly went with the Kellys to the big bonfire, the trees along the way had signs hanging on them.

KEVIN MOE — THE WAY TO GO!

VOTE FOR WHITE, HE'S ALL RIGHT!

Molly laughed.

Buddy came walking up to her.

"Do you want to be Pee Wee Scout of the Year?" she asked him.

"Naw," he said. "I don't like politics."

Buddy offered Molly half of his ice cream sandwich.

Scouts were coming out of all the tents for the big bonfire. Waves and waves of Scouts. They wore their kerchiefs and badges.

"This is going to be a big bonfire," said Mr. Baker. "It will take lots and lots of wood."

The Scouts gathered wood. They piled it high. Mr. Reed lit the fire, and soon it blazed brightly.

Then everyone gathered around in a circle. It was getting dark. The stars were shining in the evening sky overhead. Molly could hear the wind whistling in the trees.

There were Pee Wee Scouts everywhere she looked.

The Kellys sat down in a soft patch of grass. Molly sat between Mary Beth and Mr. Kelly. Buddy sat next to them, with his mother. Sonny and Mrs. Betz sat right behind the Kellys.

"I want a swimming pool," Sonny was saying to his mother.

"I don't think so," said Mrs. Betz. "It is too cold where we live to have a pool."

"We could have one inside," Sonny argued. "Please, Mom?"

Mary Beth and Molly giggled. The fire crackled and popped. It made them warm.

"Now," said Mr. Reed. "I have a surprise. We have a new song to sing tonight. A special song for the Pee Wee Jubilee."

He passed papers out to the large group. The Scouts had to read them by firelight. First the leaders sang the song out loud. They sang it twice. Then the Pee Wees joined in.

♪   ♪   ♪ The Pee Wee Jubilee ♪ ♪ ♪
                    (to the tune of "Row, Row,
                        Row Your Boat")

Come, come, come and join
Our big family.
From west, from east, we hurry to
    meet at
The Pee Wee Jubilee.

Pee Wee Scouts are here
To sing and work and play.
Meet new Scouts, find out about
The Pee Wee Jubilee.

Hold, hold, hold my hand,
Tell a story to me.
Soon it will end, but I made a new
    friend
At the Pee Wee Jubilee.

It was beautiful. They sang the song in a round, over and over.

Mr. Kelly put one arm around Mary Beth and one arm around Molly. The fire flickered and snapped. Rat's knees, Molly felt good.

Soon everyone in the big circle was holding hands and swaying back and forth like the branches of a tree. Molly felt like grabbing everyone and hugging them. She felt bigger and older now.

" 'Soon it will end, but I made a new friend at the Pee Wee Jubilee,' " she sang.

It might end, but Molly would remember this night and all her friends around the bonfire forever.

CHAPTER 8

The Pee Wee Scout Spirit

The next morning some banging noise woke Molly up. It sounded like a drum.

Bang! Bang! Bang!

When she got up and looked out of the tent she saw Kevin beating on an old pan. On his back was a sign saying VOTE MOE!

After breakfast the Scouts voted. Mr. Reed passed out little pieces of paper and little pencils. The mothers and leaders

helped the Scouts spell names. They each wrote down one name. A girl named Lucy did cartwheels around the dining hall to get people to notice her. She reminded Molly of Rachel.

Buddy said, "I'm going to vote for Ted. He's in our troop."

Mary Beth said, "I don't know whether to vote for Roger or Kevin."

"They both think they are going to win." Molly laughed. She remembered back to February. Kevin had sent her a secret valentine. And he was cute.

She voted for Kevin. "Let's go, Moe!" she shouted.

Kevin smiled at her.

While the votes were being counted, some of the Scouts played volleyball. Some entered a quick sack race.

"Will you write to me?" Molly asked Buddy.

"Sure," said Buddy. The jelly from his

donut was running down his wrist. "I don't know how to write too well, but I can print. We don't do cursive yet."

"Will you write to *me*?" demanded Sonny.

Buddy nodded. "I might even call you on the telephone, you guys," he said.

"We can visit each other!" said Sonny. "I can swim in your pool until I get one myself." He looked at his mother.

"Maybe our troops can be pen pals," said Molly. "I think there's a badge for writing to a pen pal."

Mrs. Peters called Troop 23 back to the dining hall.

"The votes are counted," she said.

"I bet I win," said Kevin.

"No way," said Roger. "I ran a good campaign."

"There were a lot of popular Pee Wees," said Mr. Reed when they were all there.

"But we added up the votes. We have the winner for you."

Roger sat on the edge of his chair. Kevin just leaned back as if he weren't worried.

Troop 23 sat very still.

"The winner is . . ." read Mr. Reed.

Just as he said the name, someone coughed. All that Troop 23 could hear was "White."

"Yeah!" shouted Roger, and jumped up off his chair. The chair fell over and made a loud noise. Troop 23 cheered, even Kevin. Roger stood by Mr. Reed, smiling.

But there was another boy standing on the other side of Mr. Reed.

He was smiling too.

Mr. Reed looked puzzled. "Which one of you boys is Robert White?" he asked.

"I am!" they both answered.

Mr. Reed frowned. "You're both Robert White?"

"Didn't you call Roger White?" asked Roger.

"I'm sorry, I called Robert White," said Mr. Reed.

Roger turned red.

"He won't sit down!" whispered Patty.

Roger just stood next to Mr. Reed and smiled a silly smile. Finally Roger's father had to go and get him.

"I thought he said Roger," mumbled Roger. "I know he did."

"I never thought both of us would lose," said Kevin.

"We are used to always having a winner in our troop," said Mrs. Peters.

"It's because we're the best troop," said Kevin.

"It's because we have never had so much competition," said Mrs. Peters.

The Scouts had to admit she was right. The world was full of other Pee Wee Scouts. They weren't the only ones.

Mr. Reed was putting a medal around Robert White's neck.

"Yeah!" shouted all the Scouts. They whistled and stamped their feet and cheered. Roger and Kevin cheered the loudest for Robert White.

After the election there was a treasure hunt. A Pee Wee Scout from Alaska won. But someone from Buddy's troop came in second, and Tim Noon came in third. Troop 23 hoisted Tim up on Mr. Kelly's shoulders and cheered some more.

"It's almost over!" cried Rachel. "The Jubilee is almost over."

"I'm afraid so," said Mrs. Peters. "It is time to pack our things and say good-bye."

Inside the Kellys' tent, Molly wrapped her sugar bowl in her pajamas so that it wouldn't break. She packed it very carefully.

Before they got on the bus for the airport,

the Scouts gathered in front of the dining hall for the last time. It was Sunday afternoon. All the Scouts and parents held hands in a big circle. The last big circle.

"I want a swimming pool," Sonny said to Mrs. Betz.

"You can ask the tooth fairy for your wish," she said. "The next time you lose a tooth."

"That's no fair!" Sonny shouted. "I never get what you say I'll get.'"

Mrs. Betz just said, "Hush."

"Yeah," whispered Roger. "Hush your face."

Patty and Lisa giggled.

The Jubilee song started again.

" 'Hold, hold, hold my hand,' " sang Molly. She gave Mary Beth's hand a squeeze. She loved her best friend. And she loved her new friend too. Buddy's address was in her pocket.

" 'Soon it will end, but I made a new friend at the Pee Wee Jubilee,' " they sang.

Mr. Reed made a little good-bye speech. He talked about helping others, reaching out, sharing and exploring. When he talked about new talents and abilities, Molly thought of her sugar bowl. She smiled. Her parents would be proud of her.

Mr. Reed was finishing his speech. ". . . and the Jubilee was a big success. Every one of you should be the Pee Wee Scout of the Year. Get home safely and keep that Pee Wee Scout spirit alive!"

Molly smiled.

The Pee Wee Scout spirit.

That's what it's all about.

Pee Wee Scout Song
(to the tune of "Old MacDonald Had a Farm")

Scouts are helpers, Scouts have fun,
Pee Wee, Pee Wee Scouts!
We sing and play when work is done,
Pee Wee, Pee Wee Scouts!

With a good deed here,
And an errand there,
Here a hand, there a hand,
Everywhere a good hand.

Scouts are helpers, Scouts have fun,
Pee Wee, Pee Wee Scouts!

☆ Pee Wee Scout Pledge ☆

We love our country
And our home,
Our school and neighbors too.

As Pee Wee Scouts
We pledge our best
In everything we do.